Jane Goodall

Doctor White

with Pictures by Julie Litty

minedition

It was a cold, wet morning.

Dr. White dashed to the hospital.

He was late.

He slipped through the back door of the kitchen.

The cook saw Dr. White first. Without saying a word, she grabbed a towel and rubbed his shaggy head.

"Where have you been? I saved your breakfast, but you'd better hurry. Mark was worse during the night.

The nurses have already been down here asking for you!"

Dr. White quickly slurped his warm tea made with milk and sugar
and hastily swallowed his buttered toast.
Without wiping his mouth, he ran up the stairs and down the
corridor on the left.
Several doctors and nurses greeted him as he passed.

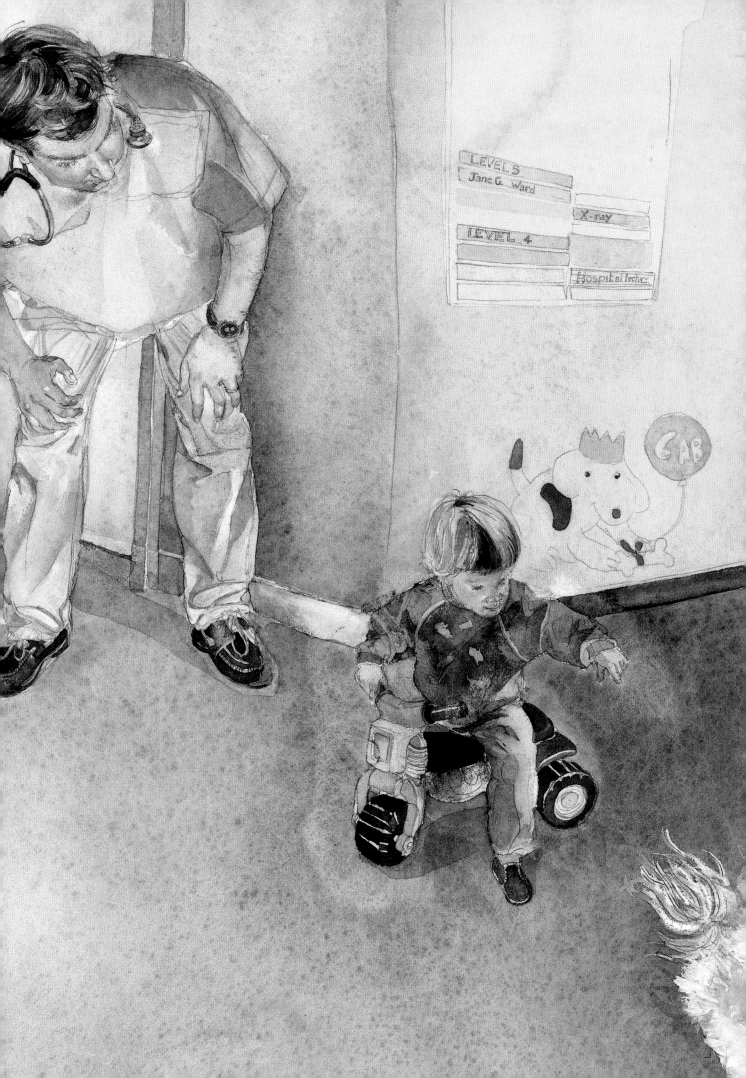

Dr. White paused at the
door before going in.
Mark's face was pale.
His eyes were closed
and he lay still.
Mark's mother was
sitting by the bed
and she was crying.

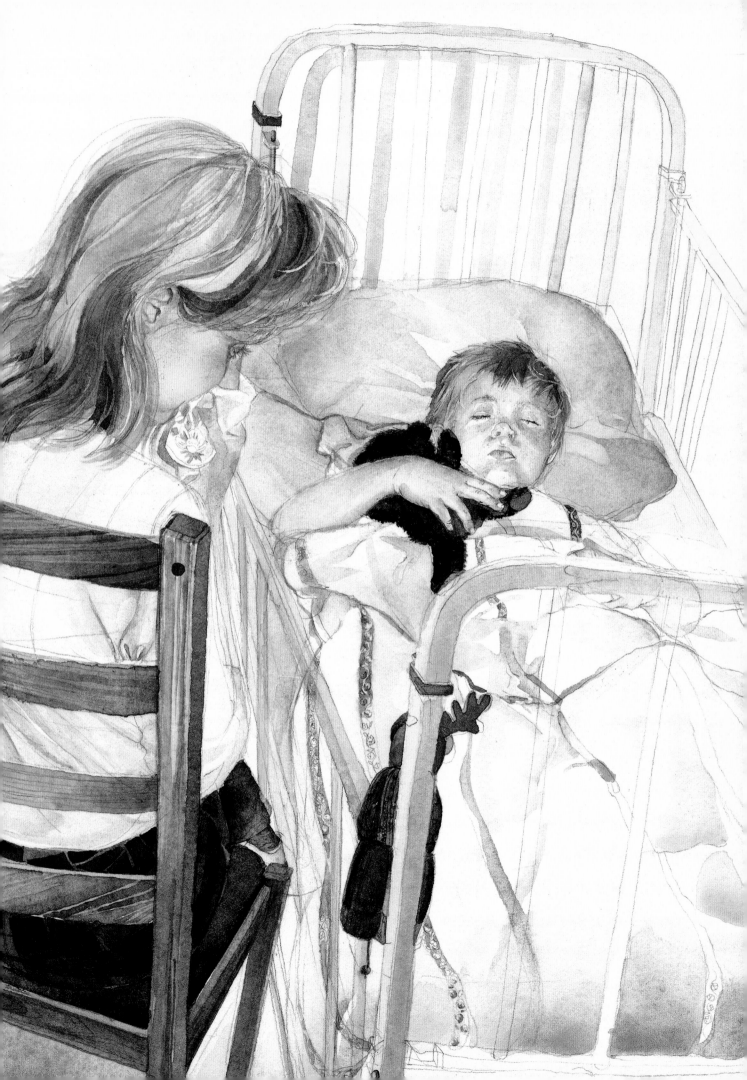

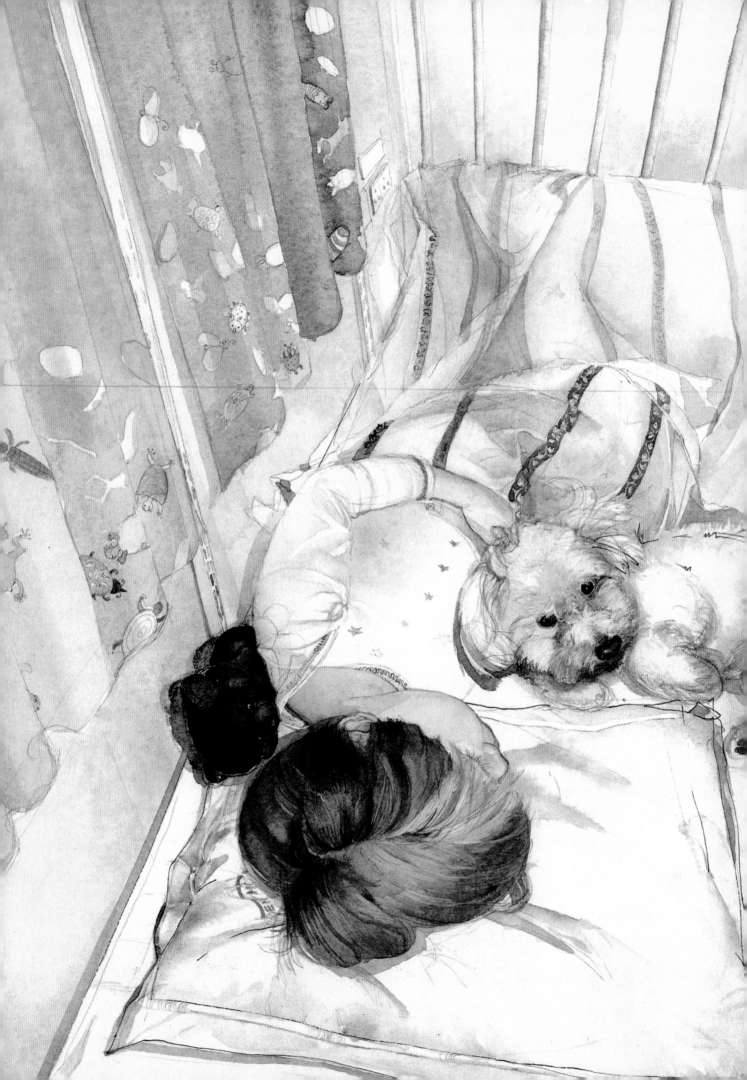

When Mark's mother saw Dr. White come in, she smiled with
relief. Dr. White jumped on the bed and curled up close to Mark.
He licked Mark's hand to let him know he was there.
Mark opened his eyes a little and smiled.
Mark's mother relaxed. She believed in Dr. White's tail-wagging
treatment. She kissed her son and patted Dr. White on the head.
"Look after him for me," she said. Then she went out for a while.

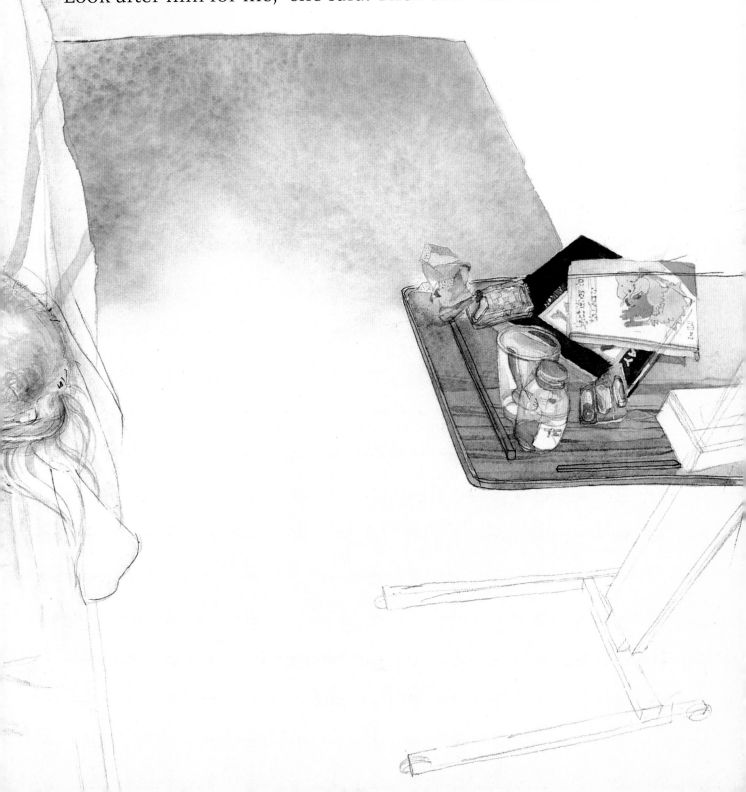

Day after day the little white
dog visited the wards of the
hospital. He wagged his tail
and looked at the children
with his soft brown eyes.
Sometimes he nudged them
with his cold black nose.
He always seemed to know
when a child was very ill.

Then, he would jump on the bed
and curl up close to them.
He would lie there for hours, licking their
hands now and then, and thumping his tail.

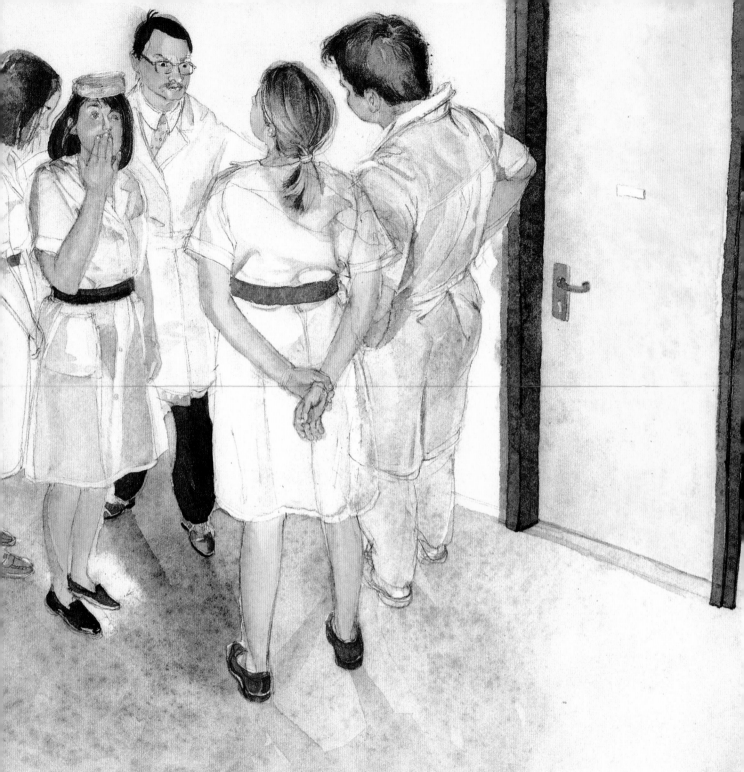

One day as Dr. White was making his rounds, he passed a man with a very red face.

The man began shouting for the nurse.

"There's a dog in the ward! There's a dog!"

The ward nurse quickly tried to explain.

"He's a very special dog. He has saved many lives!"

The man turned out to be the health inspector and he wouldn't
listen to a word the nurse said.
He reported the hospital immediately. It was official.
Dr. White was no longer allowed to visit his patients.

Day after day, the little dog curled up on the step outside the door to the kitchen. His brown eyes were sad and he never wagged his tail.

The children missed him.
Many of them weren't
getting better, and some
were getting worse.
Mark had been one of the
lucky ones. Dr. White had
worked his magic on him.
He had recovered and gone
home.

RESERVE AU
PERSONNEL

Months after Mark had left the hospital,
the health inspector returned. The head
nurse met him in the hallway.
"I suppose you're here to snoop again?"
she said bitterly. "Well, you needn't worry.
The dog doesn't come here any more
and my patients are suffering."

She looked at the inspector and saw
tears rolling down his cheeks.
"I'm afraid my little girl is very ill."
His voice broke. "Won't you
please come and see her?"
The nurse followed him down
the corridor to the ward
where the most ill children
were cared for.

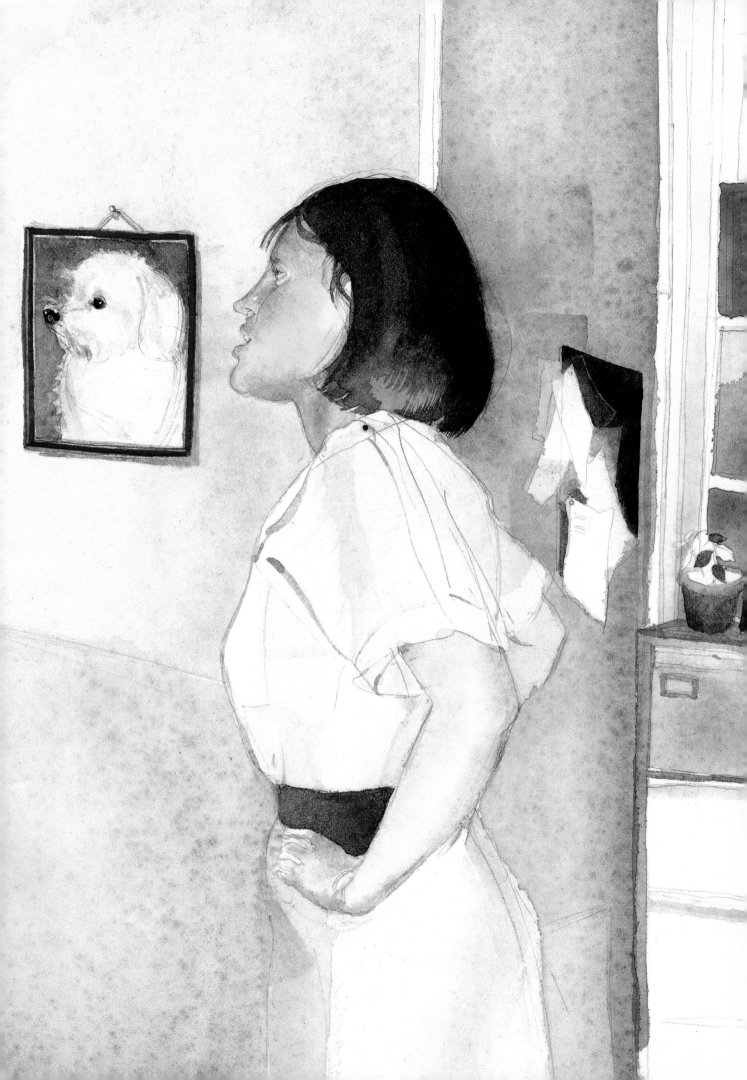

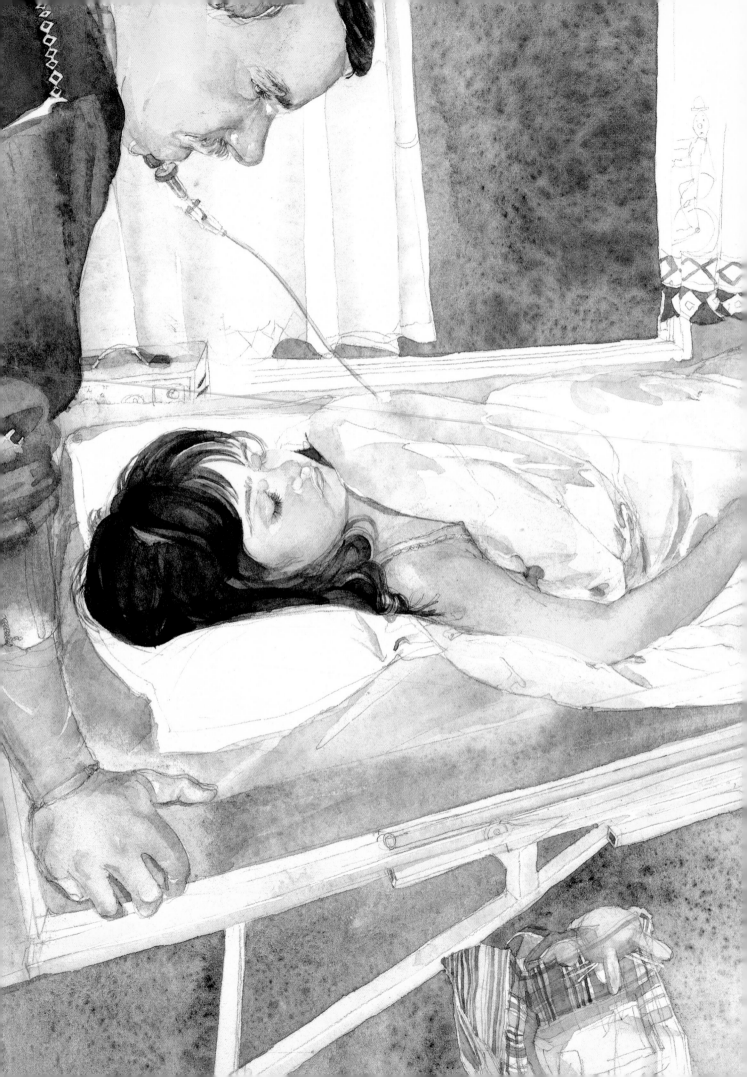

There lay a young child. Her father spoke
to her but she did not open her eyes.
"Please get better. I need you," he whispered
as his tears fell on to the child's face.
The little girl didn't respond to his words.

The head nurse thought about Mark. He had been in this same room.
Day after day the little white dog had curled up beside him on the bed.
Slowly, miraculously, Mark had recovered.
The nurse looked at the despairing father.
"We'll do all we can for your daughter," she said.

That night, the nurse went down to the kitchen.
She opened the back door.
Dr. White was curled up on the doorstep.
His brown eyes were sad, but he gave her a little welcome
with his tail. She held the door open, inviting him inside.
He leapt up and trotted through the kitchen.
Up the stairs, down the corridor.

Dr. White stood in the doorway of the little girl's
room. Her face was pale.
Her eyes were closed and she lay very still.
Dr. White jumped on the bed and curled up close
to her. His cold black nose touched her hand,
but she still didn't move.
Gently, he licked her hand from time to time to
let her know he was there.

The next morning when the health inspector came to the hospital room he saw the little white dog curled up next to his daughter.

As Dr. White thumped his tail, the little girl opened her eyes and smiled at her father. Reaching out to stroke the little white dog, the health inspector thanked him for helping his daughter get better.

No one will know how many lives the little white dog helped save, but a story is told that it was the health inspector himself who moved Dr. White's bowl back into the kitchen.

From that day forward, Dr. White was welcome at the hospital.

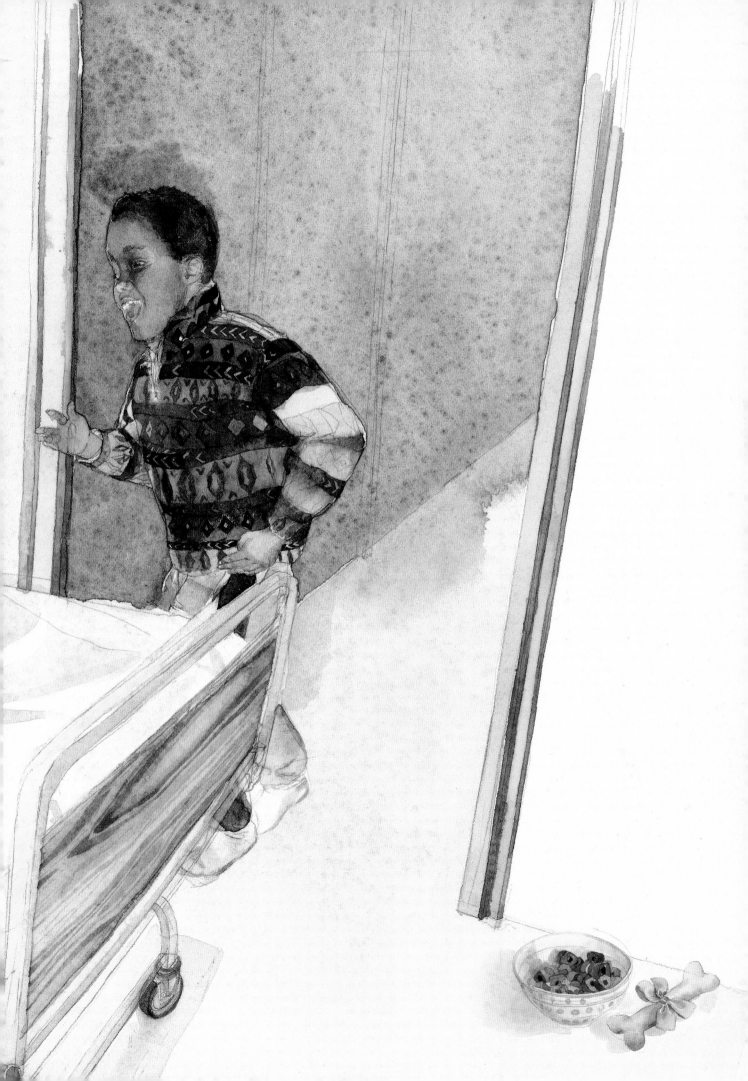

25
16
17